THE NINE FLORA McFLIMSEY BOOKS

Miss Flora McFlimsey and the Baby New Year

Miss Flora McFlimsey's Birthday

Miss Flora McFlimsey's Christmas Eve

Miss Flora McFlimsey's Easter Bonnet

Miss Flora McFlimsey's Halloween

Miss Flora McFlimsey and Little Laughing Water

Miss Flora McFlimsey and the Little Red Schoolhouse

Miss Flora McFlimsey's May Day

Miss Flora McFlimsey's Valentine

Miss Flora McFlimsey's Easter Bonnet

BY MARIANA

Lothrop, Lee & Shepard Books   New York

E
J

ILLUSTRATIONS BY MARIANA RECREATED BY CAROLINE WALTON HOWE.

Copyright © 1951, 1979 by Lothrop, Lee & Shepard Co., 1987 by Erik Bjork.

First Edition   1 2 3 4 5 6 7 8 9 10

Library of Congress Cataloging in Publication Data
Mariana.   Miss Flora McFlimsey's Easter bonnet.
Summary: Miss Flora McFlimsey remembers the day when Peterkins the rabbit brought her her first Easter bonnet. [1. Easter—Fiction. 2. Dolls—Fiction] I. Title. PZ7.M33825Mj 1987   [E]   86-15268
ISBN 0-688-04535-9   ISBN 0-688-04536-7 (lib. bdg.)

Diana was unpacking Miss Flora McFlimsey's trunk.
She was looking for Miss Flora's spring jacket and her
lightweight underwear and her white silk mitts.

Diana liked to look through Miss Flora McFlimsey's trunk. She always found something in it that she didn't remember ever having seen before. This time she felt something round and stiff. She pulled it out. It was a doll's straw hat—an odd little hat with two stiff feathers, some flowers, and a bit of ribbon on it.

"Well," said Diana, "I certainly don't remember ever seeing *that* before."

Miss Flora McFlimsey was staring at the little hat, too. There was a faraway look in her eyes.

Diana put the hat on Flora McFlimsey's head. Then
she ran downstairs to find her little sister, Toto.

Miss Flora McFlimsey continued to stare out of the window. She was thinking of another spring afternoon, long ago.

For Miss Flora McFlimsey had not always been Diana's doll. Once she had belonged to another little girl—a little girl who wore red-topped shoes and who owned a real dollhouse big enough to stand up in.

The little house had stood under the big apple tree.

  It had real furniture in it
and tiny dishes
 and a piano,

and Miss Flora McFlimsey had lived in it.

There were other dolls, too—

Genevieve

and Topsey

and Gigi,

and a rag doll named Francesca

and Little Bo-Peep

and a sheep named Baa.

The little girl in the red-topped shoes

really loved Miss Flora McFlimsey best of all, but she was careful not to let the others know it. In fact, she was just a little bit more strict with her than with the others, for that very reason.

One soft spring afternoon the door of the dollhouse was open. The dolls were watching a frisky rabbit named Peterkins hop across the lawn. The big apple tree was in bloom.

Suddenly the little girl appeared in the doorway.

She was carrying a large sewing basket full of ribbons and laces and pieces of silk and calico.

"All the dolls—and Baa," she said, "please pay attention. There's going to be an Easter party—lots of dolls are coming, and there'll be prizes for the best costumes. You'll all have to have new things, and there are only three days left to make them."

She sat right down on the floor and began cutting and sewing.

For the next three afternoons the dollhouse was a busy place. The little girl worked very hard. First she made Topsey a green and red bandanna and a new dress of yellow calico. She made Francesca an apron and a hat with poppies on it.

She trimmed a silk bonnet for Genevieve, who had been waiting impatiently. Genevieve had a new coat, too, and new patent-leather shoes besides.

Gigi had new ruffles and a big hat. Bo-Peep had a little hat and a bow for her crook. Even Baa had a new blue ribbon for his bell, and a flower.

Topsey had
a yellow dress

Genevieve had
a silk bonnet

Francesca wore
a hat with poppies

Gigi had a big hat

and
Bo-Peep
a little
hat

Baa had
a new ribbon
for his bell

Miss Flora McFlimsey sat and watched. Soon it would be her turn. She had been longing for an Easter bonnet, and the night before she had dreamed about it—a little bonnet all covered with flowers and plumes. She could see some feathers and little rosebuds in the sewing basket.

But on the third afternoon Miss Flora McFlimsey began to grow rather anxious. Wouldn't there be anything for her?

The little girl in the red-topped shoes picked up the scraps lying on the floor. It was almost time for the supper bell to ring. "Miss Flora McFlimsey," she said, "there just isn't time to do much for you. I'll give you a new hair ribbon and wash your face and mend that ruffle on your dress—but you'll just have to go as you are. And don't sulk! I want you to be a good example to the others."

Miss Flora McFlimsey tried not to cry while her face was being washed and her ruffle mended. But after the little girl had kissed all the dolls and Baa goodnight, and had gone out and shut the door of the dollhouse behind her, Flora McFlimsey began to cry very softly to herself. If only she could run away so that she wouldn't have to go to the party.

Soon the dolls were asleep—Baa with his head on Bo-Peep's shoulder. Gigi was snoring funny little doll snores. Only Miss Flora McFlimsey was still awake.

All at once there was
a little noise outside and
two ears appeared at the
window. It was Peterkins
the rabbit. He often peeped
into the dollhouse in
the evenings to see that
everything was all right.

Peterkins sometimes got
things a little mixed. He
always said goodbye when
he came, and hello when he left.

This time he said, "Goodbye, why aren't you asleep,
Miss McFlimsey, and why are you crying?"

Now Peterkins was a very sympathetic rabbit. So Miss Flora McFlimsey told him about the Easter party the next day and the bonnet that she had hoped to wear, and how she would now have to go in her old clothes.

"Don't cry anymore, Miss McFlimsey," said Peterkins. "I have an aunt who makes hats. I was just on my way to see her. Don't budge till I come back." And before Miss Flora McFlimsey could say a word, he was gone.

Miss Flora McFlimsey waited. She waited a long time. Then she heard a little rustling outside, and there was Peterkins again at the window. The moon was shining brightly. Peterkins was holding a little box between his front paws. Tied to it was a card. It said, "A Happy Easter from Peterkins' aunt—"

"It's for you," said Peterkins. "Open it."

Miss Flora McFlimsey was trembling so that she could hardly untie the strings. She raised the lid. Then she gave a little gasp. Inside the box was a doll's hat almost exactly like the one in her dream.

There was only one difference: on each side of the crown of the hat there was a round hole.

"My aunt said that the holes are for your ears to come through," explained Peterkins.

Miss Flora McFlimsey looked a little startled, but she put on the hat. "Thank you, thank you, Peterkins! And please thank your aunt."

"I'm glad you like it," said Peterkins. "My aunt said to hurry back because we'll have a busy day tomorrow. So, hello," and with that his ears disappeared.

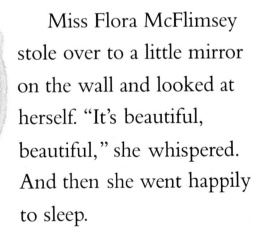

Miss Flora McFlimsey stole over to a little mirror on the wall and looked at herself. "It's beautiful, beautiful," she whispered. And then she went happily to sleep.

Everyone woke up very early the next morning. It was the day of the party.

The dolls were surprised to see Miss Flora McFlimsey wearing a new hat.

"It looks rather strange with that old dress and those shoes," remarked Genevieve.

"And what funny holes it has in it," she went on. "Why, it looks as if it were made for a rabbit!" She laughed.

Miss Flora McFlimsey began to feel quite uncomfortable in her new hat. It had seemed so beautiful in the moonlight the night before that she had hardly thought about the two holes.

Just then the little girl came hurrying in. She had been helping to hide Easter eggs on the lawn and her cheeks were pink.

She saw Miss Flora McFlimsey's hat, but she didn't have time to wonder about where it had come from, or else she was too excited to think much about it.

She found two fluffy little plumes and put one in each of the holes that Peterkins' aunt had left for ears.

Then she gathered all the dolls and Baa in her arms and carried them out under the big apple tree.

The guests were beginning to arrive.

Gigi was put next to a lovely doll dressed as a May
Queen. A baby doll in long skirts sat on Francesca's lap.
Baa was tied safely with a ribbon to Bo-Peep's crook.

Topsey sat between twin dolls in kilts and Scotch caps.
Genevieve and Miss Flora McFlimsey sat on either side of
a tall soldier named General Jackson.

Then the Easter egg hunt began, and the dolls were left alone to entertain their guests.

"I like soldier dolls," said Genevieve to General Jackson. General Jackson said nothing.

"I'm a real wax doll," she added, "and very expensive." General Jackson was silent.

"Have you noticed my new Easter bonnet?" asked Genevieve. General Jackson did not answer.

One of Miss Flora McFlimsey's feathers was tickling General Jackson's ear. At last he spoke. "What I would like to know," he said, "is who is under the hat on my left?"

"I don't think anyone is under it," said Genevieve quickly.

"There must be," said General Jackson, "because I can see the tips of two shoes."

"Perhaps it's a rabbit with shoes on," said Genevieve.

"I am under the hat, sir," said Miss Flora McFlimsey timidly.

"It is a very pretty hat," said General Jackson. "But would you mind looking up so that I can see who you are?"

Miss Flora McFlimsey looked up. General Jackson smiled down at her, and Miss Flora McFlimsey smiled back.

It was the lovely May Queen doll who won the prize for the most beautiful costume, and Baa who won the prize for the funniest—although, of course, he wasn't a doll, and as he'd stolen Bo-Peep's hat, it wasn't really his

costume either. Still, everyone seemed satisfied. But the prize for the most original costume went to the doll wearing the hat with the two feathers standing up straight like an Easter bunny's ears—Miss Flora McFlimsey.

And what was the prize? Miss Flora McFlimsey couldn't quite remember—it had all happened such a long time ago.

Perhaps it was that little bottle of Eau de Cologne in her trunk, or her lace parasol.

Miss Flora McFlimsey's thoughts came suddenly back to the present. Someone was coming. She sat up straight. The door opened, and in came Diana, followed by Toto.

"There's going to be an Easter party under the big apple tree," Diana was saying.